# THE KID WHO ONLY HIT HOMERS

★

# READ ALL THE BOOKS

## In The

## New MATT CHRISTOPHER Sports Library!

**THE BASKET COUNTS**
978-1-59953-212-7

**THE KID WHO ONLY HIT HOMERS**
978-1-59953-107-6

**CATCH THAT PASS!**
978-1-59953-105-2

**LONG-ARM QUARTERBACK**
978-1-59953-114-4

**CENTER COURT STING**
978-1-59953-106-9

**MOUNTAIN BIKE MANIA**
978-1-59953-108-3

**THE COMEBACK CHALLENGE**
978-1-59953-211-0

**RETURN OF THE HOME RUN KID**
978-1-59953-213-4

**DIRT BIKE RACER**
978-1-59953-113-7

**SKATEBOARD TOUGH**
978-1-59953-115-1

**DIRT BIKE RUNAWAY**
978-1-59953-215-8

**SNOWBOARD MAVERICK**
978-1-59953-116-8

**THE GREAT QUARTERBACK SWITCH**
978-1-59953-216-5

**SNOWBOARD SHOWDOWN**
978-1-59953-109-0

**THE HOCKEY MACHINE**
978-1-59953-214-1

**SOCCER HALFBACK**
978-1-59953-110-6

**ICE MAGIC**
978-1-59953-112-0

**SOCCER SCOOP**
978-1-59953-117-5

The New

# MATT CHRISTOPHER

## Sports Library

# THE KID WHO ONLY HIT HOMERS

NORWOOD HOUSE PRESS

CHICAGO, ILLINOIS

**Norwood House Press**
P.O. Box 316598
Chicago, Illinois 60631

For information regarding Norwood House Press, please visit our website at:
www.norwoodhousepress.com or call 866-565-2900.

**This edition was published in 2007.**


**Library of Congress Cataloging-in-Publication Data:**
Christopher, Matt.
  The kid who only hit homers.
    p. cm. -- (The new Matt Christopher sports library)
  Summary: A boy becomes a phenomenal baseball player one summer when a
mysterious stranger resembling Babe Ruth befriends him.
  ISBN-13: 978-1-59953-107-6 (library : alk. paper)
  ISBN-10: 1-59953-107-0 (library : alk. paper)  1. Large type books. (1. Baseball--Fiction.
2. Large type books.)  I. Title.
  PZ7.C458Ki 2007
  (Fic)--dc22


Printed in the United States of America

for my son,
Dale

## Author's Note

This story was told to the author by a person whose expressed wish is that he remain anonymous. Every word in it is true (so he said), except that names have been changed to protect the innocent (and those not so innocent).

The author was left to form his own opinion on whether the incidents have actually happened, and he prefers to keep that opinion to himself.

It is left to the judgment of the reader whether he wishes to do likewise.

Matt Christopher

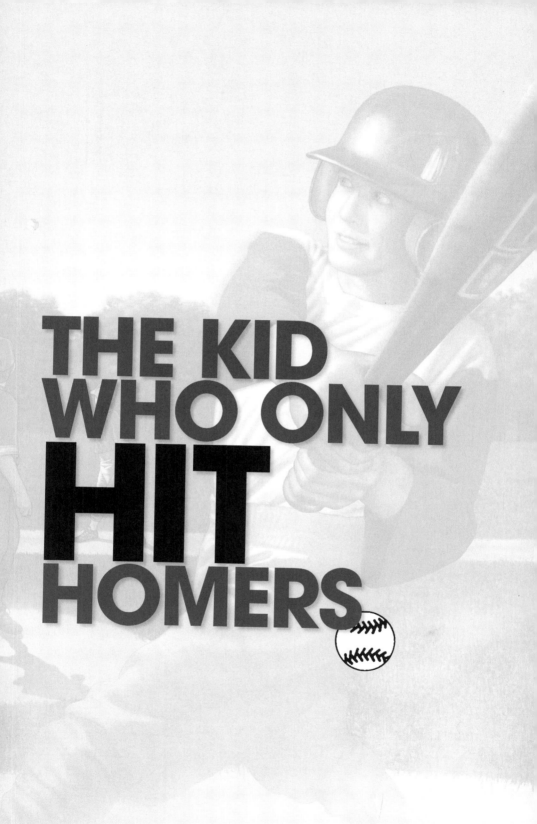

# 1

The Hooper Redbirds were having their third practice session of the spring season, and Sylvester Coddmyer III, a right-hander, was batting.

Rick Wilson hurled in the first pitch. It looked good and Sylvester swung.

Swish! He missed it by six inches.

"Just meet it, Sylvester," advised Coach Stan Corbin. "You're trying to kill it."

Sylvester tried to "just meet" Rick's next pitch and fouled it to the backstop screen. He hit the next one to Rick. It was a dribbler that took almost five seconds to reach the mound.

"Hold it up for him, Rick!" shouted Jim Cowley, the Redbirds' second baseman.

"Think that would help, Jim?" yelled Jerry Ash.

A rumble of laughter broke from the other players on the field. Sylvester didn't let it bother him, though. He was pretty used to it by now.

"Okay, Sylvester," said the coach. "Lay it down and run it out."

Sylvester bunted Rick's next pitch down to third and beelined to first base. His stocky build and short legs didn't exactly help him be a very fast runner.

He had hoped that by now he would show some improvement in his playing. If there was any, it was so slight no one seemed to notice.

His performance in the outfield wasn't any better than it was at the plate. Mr. Beach, the assistant coach, was knocking flies out to the outfielders, and Sylvester missed three out of four that were hit to him.

"Remind me to bring you my mom's clothes basket at the next practice," said Ted Sobel, one of the outfielders who was sure to make the starting lineup. "Maybe *then* you can catch it."

"Funny," said Sylvester. "Ha ha."

Twenty minutes later practice was over. The boys walked tiredly to the locker room, showered, and went home.

"Well, are you going to sign up to play?" asked Jim Cowley.

"Tomorrow the last day to sign up?"

"That's right."

"I'll think about it," said Sylvester.

He thought about it at the supper table, on the swing in the yard, and in bed before he fell asleep, and decided he wouldn't sign up. He was sure he'd just sit on the bench, anyway. And who'd like to sit on the bench all the time?

The next afternoon he sat in the bleachers and watched the Hooper Redbirds practice. No one seemed to miss him on the field. No one, that is, except Jim Cowley, who ran over from first base after batting practice.

"Syl! Why aren't you on the field?"

"I didn't sign up," answered Sylvester.

"Why not?"

Sylvester shrugged. "Why? To warm the bench? Anyway, I don't care that much about playing."

"Then why are you here?"

"Nothing else to do," replied Sylvester.

"I bet," said Jim, and ran back to the in-field.

Sylvester folded his hands over his knees, glad that Cowley had left. The guy was starting to get on his nerves.

"Why did you lie to the boy, Syl?" said a voice.

Startled, he looked and saw a man climb up the bleachers and sit beside him. He had never seen the man before, but figured he must be the father of one of the players.

He blushed.

The man smiled and put out his hand. Sylvester put his into it and felt the man's warm grip. "I'm George Baruth," said the man. "You're Sylvester Coddmyer the third, aren't you?"

"Yes, I am," said Sylvester, and frowned. George Baruth? There was no Baruth going to Hooper Junior High that he knew of. "Are . . . are you looking for me?"

George Baruth's blue eyes crinkled at the corners. He was a big man with a round face and a nose like a large strawberry. He was wearing a coat over a thin white jersey, brown pants, and a baseball cap with the letters *NY* on the front of it.

"Well, hardly," said George Baruth. "I just figured you'd be here."

Sylvester heard a sharp *crack!* and looked just in time to see catcher Eddie Exton blast a pitch over short.

"Why did you lie to the boy, Syl?" George Baruth asked again. "You do want to play baseball with the team, don't you?"

Sylvester nodded, thinking: *How could he know that? He never saw me before.* "Yes, I do," he admitted.

"Well, don't lie about it. You didn't fool Jim, and" — he grinned broadly — "you don't fool me."

Sylvester's smile didn't quite match Mr. Baruth's. He tried to think of something to say, but couldn't. He never was much of a talker.

"Syl," said Mr. Baruth, "I don't like to see a boy watch a game from the bleachers while his heart bleeds to play."

"But I would never make a ballplayer, Mr. Baruth," said Sylvester, hopelessly. "Ballplayers are good catchers and good hitters, and I don't fit into that picture at all."

"Well, you've played *some* baseball, haven't you?"

"Yes. Some."

"Okay. Stick around after the Redbirds finish their practice."

Sylvester stared at him. "Why?"

"I'm going to teach you to become a better baseball player, that's why. As a matter of fact . . ." and now Mr. Baruth's eyes twinkled, "I think I'll teach you to become one of the best players ever to play in Hooper!"

Sylvester's eyes popped. "How are you going to do that, Mr. Baruth?"

George Baruth chuckled. "You'll see, my boy. See you after practice."

He got up and left the bleachers, and once again Sylvester Coddmyer III was by himself. He kept watching the Hooper Redbirds practice hitting, and then watched the coach knock grounders to the infielders. But all the time he kept thinking about George Baruth and his promise.

*He's just pulling my leg,* thought Sylvester. *Nobody in the world could ever help me become a good ballplayer.*

Sylvester looked over his shoulder, expecting to see Mr. Baruth getting into a car or walking on the sidewalk. The man was nowhere in sight.

*He sure can vanish fast,* thought Sylvester, and turned his attention back to the practice session.

Finally the Redbirds were finished and left the field. All except Jim Cowley. He came over and looked at Sylvester. "Practice is over, Syl. Aren't you going home?"

"In a little while," replied Sylvester.

Jim frowned, then smiled. "Well, just make sure you don't stay all night. So long."

No sooner had he left than George Baruth came around the bleachers. He was carrying a baseball bat and a glove, and his coat pockets were filled with baseballs.

"Here, take the bat," said Mr. Baruth, tossing it to Sylvester. "And walk over to the backstop screen. I'll pitch to you."

Syl caught the bat, trotted to the backstop screen, and Mr. Baruth approached the small, worn area between home plate and the pitcher's mound. It was the same spot the Redbird pitchers had used during batting practice.

Syl stood at the left side of the plate

9

facing Mr. Baruth who, he saw, was left-handed.

"Keep the toes of your feet parallel with the plate," advised Mr. Baruth. "Hold your bat a few inches off your shoulder. That's right. Okay. Here we go."

He wound up and delivered. The ball came in moderately fast, heading for the plate. Sylvester swung. *Crack!* The ball blazed in a straight line to short.

"Hey! How about that?" cried George Baruth. "Nice hit!"

Sylvester smiled. He had even surprised himself!

George Baruth threw in another pitch. This one was too far inside. "Let it go!" he yelled.

Sylvester jumped back and let it go.

The third pitch blazed across the plate again, and Sylvester belted it to left center field. He hit the next to right center and the next to deep left. Now and then a pitch was too high or too wide and he would let it go. But every pitch that came over the plate he swung at and hit every time.

He couldn't understand it. Why couldn't he hit Rick's pitches as well as he did Mr. Baruth's?

After Mr. Baruth had thrown the last ball — there were eight altogether — he and Sylvester ran out to the outfield, collected them, and came back to continue the pitching and hitting.

After the fourth time of doing this, Mr. Baruth called it quits. He pushed back his cap and wiped his sweaty forehead, and Sylvester noticed his short crop of black hair with wisps of gray around the edge.

"Tomorrow tell the coach that you've changed your mind," said Mr. Baruth. "You really want to play. You have a good pair of eyes and strong, fine wrists. You're going to make a great hitter, Syl. Take my word for it."

Sylvester looked at him unbelievingly. "What about my legs, Mr. Baruth?"

"What about them? You're going to play baseball, Syl, not run in a horse race."

It wasn't till the end of the fifth period in school on Monday when Sylvester had collected enough courage to ask Coach Corbin if it was too late to sign up with the Redbirds. The coach, dressed in a brown suit, was walking toward him in the corridor.

"Oh, Co — Coach," Sylvester stammered. "Can I see you a minute, please?"

"Of course, Sylvester," said Coach Corbin, and looked at Sylvester with dark, friendly eyes. "What is it?"

"Is it too late to sign up for baseball?"

Dark brows twitched briefly, then squeezed together so that they almost touched.

"Friday was the last day to sign up, Sylvester. And I've got too many players now. Why didn't you sign up earlier? Didn't you see the notice on the bulletin board?"

"Yes. But I —" Sylvester shrugged. "Okay. Thanks, Mr. Corbin."

He walked down the corridor to his homeroom, his head bowed and his hands in his pockets. He wasn't surprised at Coach Corbin's reply. He had hoped, though, that the coach would've let him sign up. At least then he'd have had a chance to show what he could do.

After school he walked home alone. Hooper was a small town in the Finger Lakes region of New York State. Tourists drove through it all the time, but no one as much as stopped there to fill up for gas.

The school, Hooper Junior High, stood on a hill overlooking the village. Most kids lived close enough to walk to it. A few had to ride on one of the buses.

Sylvester still had two blocks to go when he heard footsteps pounding behind him, and then a familiar voice. "Syl! Wait a minute!"

He turned and there was George Baruth, running toward him.

"Oh, hi, Mr. Baruth!" he said, and stopped to wait.

George Baruth came up beside him, breathing tiredly. "Did you ask the coach?"

"Yes," said Sylvester. "He said he's got too many players now."

"I was afraid of that," said George Baruth. "Dang it, I've got to get you on the team somehow, Syl."

Sylvester looked at him. "Can't we just forget about it, Mr. Baruth? He doesn't want me to play. He probably thinks I'd just be in the way."

Mr. Baruth's eyes flashed. "That's just what we don't want him to think, Syl. We have to get him to change his mind about you and put you on the team. Now, let me think a minute."

He shoved his baseball cap back, scratched his head, and looked at the sidewalk as if among the spidery cracks he might be able to find the solution.

He started talking, but his words were low and mumbly, and Sylvester knew that he was just talking to himself.

Suddenly he jerked his cap down hard and tapped a sharp finger against Sylvester's shoulder. "I've got it, Syl!" he cried. "The team's practicing now, isn't it?"

"Yes, it is."

"Okay. Is your glove at home?"

"Yes."

"Get it, and let's go to the field. I have an idea, and it's burning a hole in my head!"

Sylvester ran the two blocks to his house, got his glove, and ran out again, yelling "Hi, Mom!" to his mother, who was stirring up something in a large bowl.

"Sylvester!" she called. "Where's the fire?"

Mom was short and blond and a little on the stocky side. Ever since Sylvester was born she had wished for a daughter, too, but so far there was only Sylvester. Dad, a traveling salesman, had said just a few nights ago that Sylvester was more than he had bargained for and that they should be thankful to have him.

"I'll be back, Mom!" Sylvester shouted over his shoulder.

Suddenly, just outside the door, he paused. He couldn't keep Mr. Baruth waiting —

not with that idea burning a hole in his head — but he had to tell Mom whom he was with.

"I'm going to be with Mr. Baruth, Mom!" he shouted to her. "He's going to help me play baseball!"

"Mr. Baruth? Who's he?"

"I don't know! But he lives in Hooper . . . somewhere! And he wants to teach me to play better baseball so that I can play with the Redbirds! He's just great, Mom! See ya later!"

He met George Baruth, and together they headed back for the school. The baseball field was south of it. The guys were already on it, taking batting practice. George Baruth climbed up the bleachers behind first base and sat down near the end of the third row. Sylvester sat beside him, wondering exactly what could be burning a hole in Mr. Baruth's head.

They sat through batting practice. Then Coach Corbin hit grounders to the infielders, and a man whom Sylvester recognized as Mr. Beach, the math teacher and Mr. Corbin's assistant coach, began hitting fly balls to the outfielders clustered in center field.

"Watch the kid in the yellow pants," said Mr. Baruth.

Sylvester watched and saw the kid misjudge one fly after another and then drop one that had fallen smack into his glove.

"That's Lou Masters," he said. "He's not doing very well, is he?"

Mr. Baruth chuckled. "He's not doing well at all, Syl. And if your coach has any sense he'd know it. Look. Run down there and ask that fella hitting the ball to let you try catching a few flies, too."

Sylvester stared at him. "But Coach Corbin told me it was too late, Mr. Baruth!"

"How can it be too late? The league doesn't start till next week. Get going. He shouldn't mind letting you try to catch a few, at least."

Reluctantly Sylvester climbed down the bleachers and walked over to Mr. Beach. He waited till Mr. Beach blasted out a fly, then gathered up all the courage he could and said, "Mr. Beach."

The tall man, windbreaker flapping in the breeze, looked at him. "Hi, Sylvester," he said. "What's up?"

"Can I . . . can I go out there, too?"

Mr. Beach smiled. "Have you signed up to play?"

"No."

"Then why do you want to go out there?"

Sylvester shrugged. "Well, I'd like to play if I can. I thought that if I did pretty good, you — or Mr. Corbin — would let me sign up."

Mr. Beach laughed. "Okay, Syl. Get out there and I'll hit you a few."

"Thank you!"

Sylvester ran out to the field, flashing a smile at George Baruth and receiving one in return. Mr. Baruth made a circle with his right thumb and forefinger.

"This one's for Syl!" yelled Mr. Beach, and hit one about as high as a ten-story building. Sylvester got under it and caught it easily.

Mr. Beach knocked out much higher flies to the other boys who seemed to have trouble judging the ball. It was Sylvester's turn again, and this time Mr. Beach hit the ball just as high as he did for the other boys. The ball soared into the blue sky until it looked no larger than a pea, came down, and dropped into Sylvester's glove.

"Hey! Nice catch, Syl!" yelled Mr. Beach. "Let's try another high one!"

He blasted another ball high into the sky. Sylvester ran some twenty feet to the spot where it was coming down, put out his mitt, and *plop!* He had it.

The other outfielders stared at him un-believingly.

"Hey! What's happened?" observed Ted Sobel. "You couldn't catch worth beans last week!"

Sylvester shrugged. "I'm not very good at it, yet," he said modestly.

After they finished outfield practice, Sylvester returned to the bleachers and sat down beside George Baruth.

"Good work, Syl," George smiled broadly. "Did you see their eyes pop when you made those fine catches?"

Sylvester grinned. "Well . . . I kind of surprised myself," he said honestly. Then he thought of something and looked at Mr.

Baruth curiously. "You're really not from Hooper, are you, Mr. Baruth?"

The big man chuckled. "No. I'm a stranger here, Syl. Every year I spend my vacation in a different town. This year I picked Hooper. This region is one of the most beautiful in the world, Syl. Did you know that?"

Sylvester smiled. "Yes, sir. I think so, too, Mr. Baruth." He paused a moment. "Mr. Baruth, how come you picked me out to help? Aren't there other kids who are better?"

Mr. Baruth chuckled again. "Why should I try to help someone who is better? I saw that you really loved baseball and tried your best to play. But you had problems. You couldn't play well, so you got discouraged and wanted to quit. Right away I knew you were a boy who needed help."

Sylvester grinned. "Do you really think you could help me, Mr. Baruth? Man, I don't think there's anybody lousier than I am."

"I not only *think* I can help you, young buddy," replied Mr. Baruth, a glimmer in his eyes. "I *know* I can!"

Suddenly there was a shout from near home plate, and Sylvester saw Coach Corbin waving to him. With the coach was Mr. Beach, who looked as if he had just uncovered a box of some very valuable treasure.

"Sylvester Coddmyer!" yelled the coach. "Come here, will you?"

"I'd better see what he wants," he said. "Excuse me, Mr. Baruth."

"You bet, Syl," said George Baruth.

Sylvester clattered down the bleachers and ran across the green, mowed grass toward the tiny group clustered near home plate. When he reached it, Coach Corbin smiled at him and placed an arm around his shoulders. "Mr. Beach told me you looked very good catching fly balls today, Sylvester," he said.

Sylvester shrugged. "I'm better at hitting, too," he said proudly.

"Oh? Mind trying to prove it to me?"

"No."

"Okay. Pick up a bat. Rick, throw a few to Sylvester."

Sylvester found a bat he liked and stepped in front of the backstop screen. Rick Wilson walked out to the temporary pitching box, waited for Sylvester to get ready, then blazed one in.

*Smack!* Sylvester laid into it and blasted it over the left field fence.

"Jumping codfish!" cried Coach Corbin. "Look at that blast! Pitch another, Rick!"

Rick did. *Pow!* The second ball rocketed out almost as far as the first. Rick threw in another. Again Sylvester swung and again the ball shot like a rocket over the left field fence.

"That's enough!" said Coach Corbin. "We can't afford to lose baseballs! Sylvester!"

"Yes, Coach?"

"I don't know what you've been doing since last Friday, but you're sure a different ballplayer now. Be in my office in the morning to sign up. I think I might be able to fit you in."

"Thanks, sir!" said Sylvester happily.

The Hooper Redbirds played a practice game with the Macon Falcons on Tuesday. Coach Corbin assigned Sylvester Coddmyer III to right field and put him fourth in the batting order. Fourth, as everybody knew, was the cleanup position.

The Redbird's batting order was:

> Cowley  2b
> Sobel  lf
> Stevens  ss
> Coddmyer  rf
> Ash  1b

Kent  cf

Francis  3b

Exton  c

Barnes  p

The Falcons had first raps. Terry Barnes, the Redbirds' alternate pitcher, was a little wild on the leadoff hitter and walked him. The next Falcon laid a neat bunt down the third-base line, which Duane Francis fielded and pegged to first on time. The bunt advanced the base runner to second, putting him in position to score.

The next Falcon blasted a fly back to Terry. Terry caught it, spun, and shot the ball to second to nab the man before he could tag up.

Three outs.

Sylvester came trotting out of right field and saw several people sitting in different places in the bleachers. And, there in the third row from the bottom just behind first base, sat Mr. Baruth.

"Hi, Mr. Baruth!" cried Sylvester.

"Hi, Syl!" answered Mr. Baruth, smiling. "Go get 'em, kid!"

Jim Cowley led off with a grounder to short, an easy out. Ted Sobel singled and Milt Stevens walked, bringing up Sylvester Coddmyer III.

"Knock 'em in, Syl!" yelled the coach.

Duke Farrel, the Falcons' tall right-hander, blazed his first pitch down the heart of the plate. Sylvester leaned into it, swung — and missed.

The next pitch was slightly high. That was Sylvester's opinion. The umpire's opinion was different. "Strike two!" he yelled.

The next pitch looked high, too. But Sylvester didn't want to take a chance on striking out. He swung. Missed!

"Strike three!"

He couldn't believe it. The first time at bat and he struck out. What would the coach think? What would Mr. Baruth think?

He turned glumly, tossed his bat onto the pile, and went to the dugout.

"Chin up, Sylvester," said the coach. "You'll be up again."

Jerry Ash popped up to short and the side retired.

The Falcons scored a run at their turn at bat, and then the Redbirds came to bat. Bobby Kent singled. Duane Francis's bunt put him on second, and Eddie Exton's triple scored him. Pitcher Terry Barnes's single scored Eddie.

The Falcon's leadoff man lambasted a long clout to deep right field, sending Sylvester running back toward the fence. His short legs were a blur as he ran, while all the time he kept his eyes on the ball. Then he reached up. The ball came down, brushed the tip of his glove, and bounced against the fence.

The Falcon ran all the way around to third on the hit.

The next hitter blasted a line drive over first baseman Jerry Ash's head. The ball struck the ground in front of Sylvester. But, instead of bouncing up into Sylvester's waiting glove, it skidded through his legs.

Once again he spun and sprinted after the ball. A run scored by the time he pegged it in.

*Man, oh, man!* he thought. *What's wrong with me? I'm not doing anything right! Mr. Baruth will give up on me for sure.*

Terry fanned the next hitter. Then Bobby caught a long fly in deep center field, and another run scored after the runner tagged up. Eddie Exton caught a pop fly to end the half inning.

"Hey, Syl," said Jim Cowley, "what're you doing out there? Playing baseball or running a track meet?"

"Ha ha," said Sylvester.

Milt Stevens led off the bottom of the third with a double over the shortstop's head. Up came Sylvester for the second time.

"Okay, Syl," said Jerry Ash, kneeling with his bat in front of the dugout. "Make up for those errors."

The pitch. It looked good. Sylvester swung. *Crack!* A long blast to center field! Sylvester dropped his bat and bolted for first, but slowed up before he got to it. The center fielder had caught the ball.

"Tough luck, kid," said a voice from the bleachers. "But don't give up. Hang in there."

Sylvester looked at Mr. Baruth. His smile

was weak. *I've got to, Mr. Baruth,* he thought, *or Coach Corbin will bench me.*

Jerry Ash singled, scoring Milt. Bobby and Duane both got out, ending the half inning. Falcons 3, Redbirds 3.

The Falcons got a man on and threatened to score when Steve Button, their cleanup hitter and a left-hander, clouted a skyscraping fly to right field. Bobby Kent started to run over from center, but Sylvester yelled, "I'll take it! I'll take it!"

"Take it!" shouted Bobby.

The ball dropped into Sylvester's glove and stuck there. A shout sprang from the scattered Redbird fans as Sylvester heaved the ball in, holding the runner on second base.

He felt much better now. He *needed* that catch.

The next two Falcons failed to hit, and the

half inning ended with a zero on the scoreboard.

"Nice catch, Syl," said Mr. Baruth as Sylvester trotted in from right field.

"Thanks, sir." Sylvester smiled.

Neither team scored again until the bottom of the fifth. With one out Sylvester socked a single, a scratch hit to shortstop. Jerry Ash's triple scored him.

Falcons 3, Redbirds 4.

"Hold 'em, Redbirds!" yelled a fan.

Terry walked the first Falcon and the next was safe on Milt's error at short. Then Steve Button blasted another fly to right field. Sylvester got under it, shouting, "I'll take it! I'll take it!"

Then, just for an instant, he lost sight of the ball against the white clouds. When he spotted it again, it was too late. The ball skimmed past his glove and struck the ground. He caught the high bounce and pegged it in, but not before two Falcons crossed home plate.

When the Redbirds came to bat, they failed to score and the game went to the Falcons, 5 to 4.

"I can't figure it out, Sylvester," said Coach Corbin, wonderingly. "You hardly looked like the same kid out there who practiced with us yesterday."

"Are — are you going to drop me, Coach?" asked Sylvester worriedly.

"No. But if you don't do better than you did today . . ." The coach shrugged. "I'll just have to keep you on the bench most of the time."

**S**ylvester Coddmyer III wrote a composition that night on snakes and how they benefit humans. It was for English. He had wanted to write on baseball because he loved it so much. But Miss Carroll, his English teacher, suggested that he write about something else for a change.

He researched his material from a couple of magazine articles and the computer. He wasn't especially crazy about snakes, but after reading up on them he realized that they were really interesting creatures.

Nevertheless, he enjoyed baseball more than anything else. He liked to read about its history, and about old-time ballplayers.

He thought of himself becoming a great outfielder or a great hitter. Man! Wouldn't that be something?

He knew he was just dreaming, though. He would never be *half* as great as any of those hitters whose names he'd read in the baseball encyclopedia.

He picked up the big book from the shelf near the desk and leafed through it to the section where the names of the home-run hitters were listed. Right on top was Babe Ruth, with 714 home runs. Man! 714!

George Herman "Babe" Ruth had been a pitcher for the Boston Red Sox. Then he went to the New York Yankees, where he played outfield and became a batting champion. He hit sixty home runs in 1927 and held the record until it was broken by Roger Maris in 1961. When he died in 1948, he held seventeen World Series records.

There were other great hitters — Willie Mays, Mickey Mantle, Jimmy Foxx. But no one had hit as many home runs as the "Babe."

Sylvester closed the book, shut his eyes, and dreamed again. Wouldn't it be something to be good enough to have *his* name in the encyclopedia some day?

He opened his eyes and laughed. He'd never!

The Hooper Redbirds' first league game was on April 28 against the Tigers from Broton. Coach Corbin assigned Sylvester to right field and put him at the bottom of the batting order.

Sylvester wasn't surprised. He felt he was lucky to be in the lineup at all.

The Redbirds batted first. They got two men on but failed to score. Sylvester trotted out to right field, hardly glancing at the fans that sat scattered in the bleachers.

The Redbird cheerleaders, wearing white sweaters and short red skirts, whooped up a cheer from the first-base bleachers side, followed by a cheer from the Tiger cheerleaders, who wore yellow jerseys and blue skirts and were at the third-base bleachers side.

Thinking of George Baruth made Sylvester look briefly at the bleachers, near the end. He really didn't expect to see Mr. Baruth there.

But he was! He was sitting at the end of the third row from the bottom, where he always sat.

The perplexed look on Sylvester's face changed to a smile. He waved, and Mr. Baruth, smiling, waved back.

Rick Wilson, on the mound for the

Redbirds, whiffed the first Tiger, then got into a hole with the second and walked him. An error by shortstop Milt Stevens, and then a clean single through the pitcher's box, scored a run before the Redbirds could smother the Tigers.

Duane Francis led off in the top of the second with a drive to center field that the fielder caught for the first out. Eddie Exton grounded out, and Rick came to bat, looking as if he were going to be the third victim for sure.

He walked on four straight balls, and up came Sylvester Coddmyer III.

Sylvester pulled on his protective helmet and stepped into position in the box. All three outfielders were standing with their legs wide apart and their arms crossed over their chests. The Tigers' infielders were making the usual noises, while, in the stands, several of the fans yawned.

"Strike one!" yelled the ump as Jim Smith blazed the first pitch over the plate.

Then, "Ball!" And "Ball two!"

He swung at the next pitch. "Strike two!"

The fans of both teams began yelling loudly. Sylvester felt sweat on his brow. Was he going to strike out and let both the coach and Mr. Baruth down? Was he going to disappoint them again?

The pitch. It headed for the inside corner. He swung.

*Crack!* A hard, solid blow! The ball shot like a white streak toward left field! And then — over the fence!

Sylvester dropped his bat and trotted around the bases for his first home run of the season.

The entire team was waiting for him behind home plate. Each member shook his hand as he crossed it.

"Nice sock, Syl!"

"Great blast, man!"

Even Coach Corbin and Mr. Beach shook his hand. "You came through that time, Syl!" exclaimed the coach, beaming.

Sylvester smiled.

Jim Cowley got up and flied out.

The Tigers went down without scoring in the bottom of the second. The Redbirds came to bat, and Jim Smith seemed to have some kind of jinx on the ball as he mowed down Sobel, Stevens, and Ash with ten pitches. The Tigers came to bat again.

Rick fired in two strikes on the leadoff batter, then got a little wild and walked him. The next Tiger bunted, advancing the runner to second and getting safely to first himself as third baseman Duane Francis muffed the wiggling grounder.

A left-handed hitter, a big kid with pants halfway down his legs and wisps of black hair sticking out from under his helmet, stepped to the plate.

Duane turned and motioned to Sylvester. "Back up, Syl! About twenty steps!"

Sylvester backed up exactly twenty steps and crouched, hoping that the guy would either strike out, hit a grounder, or knock the ball to some other field. Even though he had caught some high flies in practice, he had missed them in a practice game.

*Smack!* A high soaring fly heading for right field! Sylvester figured that it was going over his head and started to run back.

His feet slipped and down he went.

## 5

**P**anic gripped Sylvester as he looked skyward, searching frantically for the ball, which he had momentarily lost sight of.

There it was, coming right at him! Without rising to his feet — he didn't have time, anyway — he lifted his glove and made a one-handed catch.

Then he scrambled to his feet and pegged the ball into the infield. Jim Cowley caught it and quickly turned, ready to throw it. But the runners had returned to their bases — one to first, the other to second. Calmly, Jim threw the ball to Rick.

The Redbird fans cheered Sylvester for his great catch, and he blushed. It was just lucky, he thought, that he had fallen in the right spot and turned in time.

Two singles in a row scored two runs for the Tigers. Then Rick whiffed a left-handed hitter. The next blasted a triple, scoring two more runs. Eddie Exton caught a pop-up to end the inning, Redbirds 2, Tigers 5.

Bobby Kent led off in the top of the fourth.

"Come on, Bobby," said Coach Corbin. "We need runs, and the only way to get them is by getting hits."

The Tigers were a determined, fighting bunch as they kept up a steady chatter on the field. The will to win was in every move they made.

Bobby took two balls and a strike before moving the bat off his shoulder. He fouled a pitch for strike two, and the noise in the infield grew louder than ever. Then he blasted a high throw to center field that the Tiger outfielder caught without trouble.

Coach Corbin's groan could be heard throughout the Redbirds' dugout.

Duane Francis had a problem with his pants. He kept pulling them up after each swing. His third swing resulted in a sharp single over short.

"Nice hit," yelled the coach.

Eddie Exton must have looked pretty dangerous to Jim because the Tiger pitcher threw four straight balls to him, none of which was within five inches of the plate. Eddie walked.

Two men on. Only a homer could tie the score.

Rick Wilson looked dangerous, too. He seemed to be glowering at the pitcher, daring him. Sylvester knew, though, that it was just Rick's natural look whenever he came to bat.

Rick pounded out Jim's third pitch for an easy out to left field. And up came Sylvester Coddmyer III.

"Don't be too anxious, Sylvester," advised Coach Corbin. "Just a nice easy poke will be fine."

Jim Smith stepped to the mound, stretched his arms up high, brought them down, looked at the runners, then threw. The pitch blazed in. Sylvester stepped into it, saw that it was too high, and let it go.

"Ball one!" cried the ump.

Jim repeated his movements with hardly a change. This time the pitch was too far outside.

"Ball two!"

"Don't be afraid of 'im, Jim!" shouted the Tiger catcher. "He was just lucky before!"

Jim drilled the third pitch over the heart of the plate. Sylvester stepped into it and swung. He didn't know how to hit "just a nice easy poke." He swung hard, just like he had always done.

There was the solid sound of wood meeting horsehide, and then the horsehide shooting out to deep left center field, rising steadily and then falling . . . falling far beyond the fence for a home run.

The Redbird fans stood up and applauded, and the cheerleaders went crazy clapping and cheering and doing cartwheels. Sylvester trotted around the bases, shook hands with the guys waiting for him at the plate, and sat down. He hadn't even run hard enough to work up a sweat.

Jim Cowley walked, then Ted Sobel grounded out to end the half inning. Redbirds 5, Tigers 5.

Sylvester saw the coach looking at him.

Mr. Corbin's mouth hung open, but he seemed too numbed to speak.

The Tigers' leadoff man socked a scratch single past Jerry Ash, then ran to second on a sacrifice bunt. The next Tiger blasted a high fly to right field. Sylvester sprinted after it. At the last moment he dove with his glove hand stretched out. He landed on his stomach at the same time that the ball landed in his glove.

He rose quickly and winged the ball to Jerry, who sped to first base and touched it before the runner could tag up. Obviously the Tiger didn't think that the Redbird right fielder was going to get within miles of the ball.

Two outs, and a runner on second base.

Rick fired in two pitches, a strike and a ball. Then the Tiger hit one back to him, which Rick caught and tossed to Jerry for the third out.

"For a slow runner you sure can cover a lot of ground fast!" exclaimed Jim Cowley as Sylvester tossed his glove to the side of the dugout and sat down.

"I guess it just takes that extra effort," said Sylvester.

Glenn Higgins, pinch-hitting for Stevens in the top of the fifth, cracked the first pitch for a single over second base. Jerry flied out to left, and Lou Masters, pinch-hitting for Bobby Kent, walked. Duane struck out, and Eddie Exton walked, filling the bases.

The fans applauded Rick as he stepped to the plate. So far he had walked and flied out. "You're due, Rick!" shouted Jim Cowley.

Rick flied out to left field.

The Tigers came to bat, gnashing their teeth. The leadoff man waited out Rick's pitches, got two balls and two strikes on him, then drilled Rick's next pitch through the hole between left and center fields for two bases.

Milt Stevens fumbled a hot grounder, chalking up an error.

Men on first and second.

*Crack!* A sharp blow over first baseman Jerry Ash's head. Sylvester ran in a couple of steps, caught the ball on a hop, and fired it in. It was a long, hard throw, heading directly for Eddie Exton, who was crouched over home plate, waiting for it. Rick caught it instead, turned, and whipped it to Eddie just as the runner slid in between Eddie's legs.

"Out!" yelled the ump.

A grounder to third ended the threat.

"Okay, Syl," said Coach Corbin. "This is the last inning and you're first man up. What're you going to do?"

Sylvester shrugged. "I don't know. I never led off before. Shall I wait him out?"

The coach grinned. "Use your judgment, Syl. It's been working pretty good for you so far."

Sylvester smiled. "Okay, sir. Thanks."

He pulled on his helmet, picked up his favorite bat, and stepped to the plate. The stands and bleachers turned into a beehive.

Jim blazed in a pitch. Sylvester let it go, thinking it a little bit too close.

"Strike!" yelled the ump.

Sylvester let another pitch blaze by, believing it was outside.

"Strike two!" yelled the ump.

Sylvester stepped back and looked at him. The umpire smiled pleasantly. "Don't grumble, Sylvester," he said. "That cut the outside corner."

Sylvester stepped back into the box. Jim Smith's next pitch came in and looked almost exactly like the one before it. Man, he couldn't let this one go by and be called out on strikes. He swung.

*Smack!* The ball shot toward right field, climbing higher and higher the farther it went, and dropped inches on the other side of the fence. A home run.

The fans and cheerleaders went wild.

They yelled and jumped, and someone screamed, "Hold it! Ya wanna break down the bleachers?"

"You're terrific, Sylvester," commended Coach Corbin as he shook hands with Sylvester Coddmyer III. "Three homers in your first game! That's a record, son!"

Sylvester blushed. "You mean no one has hit three homers in a first game before?"

"I don't think so," said the coach. "Not for Hooper Junior High, anyway."

Jim Cowley walked, but the next three guys failed to get on and the Redbirds retired. The Tigers leadoff man flied out to center. Glen missed another hot grounder, his second, and the Tigers had a man on.

The next Tiger smashed out a single, and the runner on first dashed around to third, sliding in to the bag in a close play.

"Safe!" yelled the man in blue.

Rick fanned the next man. Two outs. Then

Rick caught a pop-up, ending the game. Redbirds 6, Tigers 5.

Sylvester picked up his glove and barely turned around to head for home when the mob swooped on him like a flock of pigeons onto a pile of corn. The shook his hands. They patted him on the back. They ruffled his hair. They praised him. He had never expected anything like this in his life.

When they finally broke away, there was one kid still standing there, smiling at him. He was much shorter than Sylvester, and younger. His hair was blond and sort of long, and he wore tinted, black-rimmed glasses.

Snooky Malone was the only kid Sylvester knew who read everything he could get his hands on about astrology. It was his belief that every person was born under a certain star and that that star ruled his destiny.

"Hi, Sylvester," said Snooky, his eyes like large black periods behind the tinted lenses.

"Hi, Snooky," said Sylvester, straightening up his clothes and his cap and starting for home.

Snooky Malone ran after him. "I was just wondering, Syl. When's your birthday? The day and month . . . I don't need the year."

Sylvester looked at him curiously. Snooky couldn't weigh over eighty-six pounds.

"What do you mean you don't need the year?"

Snooky's smile faded and came back. "I want to read your horoscope, that's why. Bet you were born under the sign of Scorpio."

"When's that?"

"Between October twenty-fourth and November twenty-second."

"Wrong," said Sylvester. "I was born between May first and May thirtieth. May twenty-seventh, to be exact."

"Gemini!" Snooky's smile brightened like a star itself.

"What's exciting about that?" asked Sylvester, not especially sharing Snooky's enthusiasm.

"It's your star! You're a Gemini!" said Snooky.

Sylvester frowned. "Is that good or bad?"

Snooky laughed. "How could it be bad? You're knocking out home runs, aren't you?"

A voice called from near the dugout. "Sylvester!" It was Coach Corbin. "I'm inviting the team to an ice cream treat at Chris an' Greens! Can you come?"

"Right now?"

"Right now."

"I'll be there," said Sylvester.

He looked around and saw Snooky running toward the gate. Then he looked toward the first-base bleachers and saw George

Baruth standing in front of them, waving to him.

"Nice hitting, Sylvester!" cried Mr. Baruth.

"Thanks!"

"Oh, that's okay, Syl. As a matter of fact, you deserve it."

Sylvester stopped dead in his tracks, turned, and saw Coach Corbin smiling at him.

It was the coach who had answered him. When he looked back toward the bleachers, George Baruth was gone.

# 7

Sylvester put down a banana split that was bigger, "bananier," and nuttier than he had ever had before. And just because he was the hero of today's game.

The team then went home. After Sylvester showered and got into clean, everyday clothes, he ate supper with Mom. Dad was out on "the road," as he called it. He wasn't coming home till Friday night.

"You probably won't want dessert after having a banana split," said Mom, whose color of eyes and hair matched his.

"What have you got?" he asked. He felt full, but if Mom had baked something he liked, he'd make room for it.

"Apple pie," she said.

Apple pie? No pie made was tastier and more delicious than the apple pie Mom made.

"I'll have a piece," he said.

His mother stared at him. "Are you sure?"

"Yes, I'm sure," he answered and settled back to wait for it.

She took the pie — a large, puffy, crusty thing — out of the oven, set it on the counter, and cut him a piece. She placed it on a small dish and put it before him. His mouth watered just looking at the soft, juicy apples oozing from under the crust.

He made a noise like a hungry tiger, cut a chunk of it with his fork, and stuck it into his mouth. While he chewed he looked up at his mother, his eyes as big as stoplights. "Mom," he said, "it tastes just as delicious as it looks!"

"Thank you, son," she said. "But don't make a hog of yourself."

Five minutes after he was finished he felt sick. Mom cleared off the table and he still sat there.

"Something wrong, Sylvester?" she asked.

"I think I made a hog of myself," he replied frankly.

"Ate too much, didn't you?"

He nodded. "Can I lie down?"

"Not on a full stomach. Sit in the living room till your food digests a bit. Later on you may lie down."

He got up, went into the living room, and sat down. He didn't even feel like turning on the television set. He sat with his legs sprawled out and his head resting against the side of the easy chair. Man, did he feel sick.

After a while Mom let him go to bed.

"You'll feel much better in an hour or so," she said.

He closed his eyes. He didn't know whether he had slept or not, but when he opened them again, there sat George Baruth, looking at him sourly.

"Hi, kid," said George.

"Well, hi, Mr. Baruth," replied Sylvester. "I didn't hear you come in. I guess I must have fallen asleep."

"I understand you overloaded yourself," said George Baruth.

Sylvester grinned weakly. "A little," he admitted.

"Little, my eye," grunted George Baruth. "If it were a little you wouldn't be lying there. First a big banana split, then a chunk of apple pie on top of a big dinner. If that isn't being a glutton I don't know what is."

"Yeah. You're right, Mr. Baruth. But how did you know I was sick? How did you know I had a banana split and then an apple pie on top of my dinner?"

George Baruth's eyes twinkled, and he reached over and patted Sylvester's hand. "Don't worry about it, kid," he said softly. "Just don't make a hog of yourself again or you'll find yourself sitting on the sidelines instead of playing."

He rose. "Take care, kid. See you at the next game."

"Okay, Mr. Baruth. Thanks for coming."

After George Baruth left, Sylvester lay there, thinking. *How did he know I was sick?* he wondered. *Only Mom knew that.*

Presently Mom came in, smiling. "Feel better?" she asked.

"Yeah." He looked at her seriously. "Mom, did Mr. Baruth call or something?"

She frowned. "Mr. Baruth?"

"Yes. He's the guy who's helping me play baseball. Did he call? Did you tell him I was sick?"

"What do you mean, Sylvester? I didn't see any Mr. Baruth."

He stared at her. "He was here a few minutes ago, Mom. You . . . you must have let him in."

She looked at him worriedly, came nearer, and put a hand on his forehead. "You're cool now," she observed. "You must have had a fever, or were dreaming."

"No, I wasn't, Mom," he insisted. "He was here, visiting me!"

The worried look disappeared and she smiled. "Okay, okay. Don't get excited. But please try to understand, son. No one came in here. I would have seen him if he did. You must have dreamed it all."

The Hooper Redbirds had first raps against the Lansing Wildcats in their second league game on the Lansing athletic field. Apparrently Coach Corbin's faith in Sylvester Coddmyer III had improved, because he was lifting Sylvester's position in the batting order from ninth to eighth.

Sylvester glanced at the first-base bleachers. Sure enough, George Baruth was sitting at the end of the third row, wearing the same pants, same jersey, same coat, same cap. Mr. Baruth must have caught his eye for he lifted a hand in a wave, and Sylvester waved back.

He thought of that evening last week when he was sick and had that dream — or whatever it was — of George Baruth's coming to visit him. If it was a dream, it sure was as real as could be.

Jim Cowley, leading off, lambasted a high pitch to center field for the first out. Ted Sobel struck out, Milt Stevens walked, and Jerry Ash flied out to end the top half of the inning.

Right-hander Terry Barnes, slender as a reed and slow as molasses, had trouble finding the plate and walked the first two Wildcats. Up came Bongo Daley, the short, stout Wildcat pitcher.

"A pitcher batting third?" muttered Jim Cowley. "Must be a hitter, too."

Apparently Bongo was. He drilled Terry's first pitch to left center for a double, scoring one run. The cleanup hitter stepped to the plate.

Terry bore down and struck him out with five pitches. Bobby Kent caught a long fly in center field. The runner on third tagged up and raced in for the second run. A pop-up to short ended the inning.

"Come on, you guys," snapped Coach Corbin. "This isn't tiddlywinks. It's baseball. Let's get going!"

Bobby, leading off, smashed a liner down the left-field foul line that just missed going fair by inches. He lambasted another almost in the same spot.

"Straighten it out, Bobby!" yelled the coach.

Bobby did. The third baseman caught the next line drive without moving a step.

The ball hadn't risen more than five feet off the ground. One out.

Duane walked. Eddie popped to short for the second out, and up to the plate stepped Sylvester Coddmyer III.

The crowd cheered. The cheerleaders led with:

*Fee! Fie! Fo! Fum!*
*We want a home run!*
*Sylvester Coddmyer!*
*Hooraaaay!*

Suddenly Sylvester remembered that he had forgotten to look for the coach's signal. He stepped out of the box, glanced at the coach sitting in the dugout, received a smile in return and the sign to "hit away," and stepped back into the box.

"Ball!" cried the ump as Bongo blazed in the first pitch.

"Ball two!"

Then, "Strike!"

*Wasn't that a little too low?* thought Sylvester.

"Ball three!"

"He's going to walk you, Syl!" yelled Jim Cowley.

"Steeeeerike!"

Three and two. Bongo caught the ball from his catcher, stepped off the mound, loosened his belt, tightened it, yanked his cap, and finally stepped on the rubber. He stretched, delivered, and *bang!*

Sylvester's bat connected with the ball, and for a moment he watched the white sphere drill a hole through the sky as it shot to deep center field. Then he dropped the bat and started his easy run around the bases while the cheers of the fans and cheerleaders rang in his ears.

"It's fantastic, Syl!" cried the coach as he

shook Sylvester's hand at the plate. "Just fantastic!"

"How do you do it?" asked Jerry Ash, who was supposed to be the team's cleanup hitter.

"I just pick the good one and swing," replied Sylvester honestly.

"And blast it out of the park," added the coach.

Terry went down on three straight pitches. Three outs.

Redbirds 2, Wildcats 2.

Terry Barnes's first pitch to the Wildcat leadoff man was drilled sharply through the hole between first and second bases. Sylvester stooped to field the low, sizzling roller, but the ball squirted through his legs. He spun, raced after it, picked it up near the fence, and heaved it in. Sick over the error, he saw the Wildcat pulling up safely at third.

"Forget to drop your tailgate, Syl?" asked Ted Sobel, grinning.

"Guess so," replied Sylvester.

A pop fly to third, and then a one-hopper slammed back to Terry, accounted for two outs, and Sylvester felt better. The Wildcat whose ball he had let skid through his legs was still on third.

Ted Sobel caught a long, high fly for the third out.

Bobby Kent belted a single that half inning, scoring two runs.

Bongo's home run over the left-field fence with nobody on was the Wildcats' only hit in the bottom of the third.

Eddie Exton, leading off for the Redbirds in the top of the fourth, popped out to second. And even before Sylvester started for the plate, the Redbird cheerleaders were yelling:

*Hey! Hey! Who do we admire?*
*Sylvester Coddmyer!*
*The third!*

The girls jumped and clapped, joined in applause by the Redbird fans.

Sylvester, blushing, stepped to the plate.

**B**ongo Daley fired the first pitch high and outside for ball one. He didn't look worried that the batter might blast a pitch out of the lot.

But the next two pitches weren't over the plate either.

His catcher called time and ran out to the mound to talk with him. So did the first and third baseman. The huddle lasted half a minute.

The guys returned to their positions, and Bongo toed the rubber again. He wound up, delivered, and the ball nipped the inside corner for a strike.

He fired another in the same spot for strike two. "You have 'im now, Bongo!" yelled the catcher.

The next pitch was almost over the heart of the plate, chest-high. Sylvester liked the looks of it and swung. The solid blow alone told the story. It was another blast over the right-field fence.

The Redbird cheerleaders and fans went wild.

It was their only run that inning. The Wildcats scored once and held the Redbirds scoreless in the top of the fifth inning with Sylvester waiting for his third trip to the plate.

Redbirds 5, Wildcats 4.

He tossed his bat aside and ran out to his position in right field, smiling and waving to George Baruth sitting in the bleachers behind first base. George smiled and waved back, but so did several other people, as if they thought that Sylvester was smiling and waving at them.

The Wildcats scored a run on an error by Milt and then a line drive over second base. Redbirds 5, Wildcats 5.

Coach Corbin was clasping and unclasping his hands, and now and then wiping his forehead with his handkerchief. He never said very much, and he seldom got angry. But he sure did get extremely nervous whenever the game was close.

And it was close now. Too close. This was the top of the sixth inning. It was their last chance to break the tie. If they couldn't, the Wildcats would get a chance to. And if they succeeded, the Redbirds would lose.

"Don't ever be ashamed to lose," the coach had once said. "Everybody loses sometimes. But play to win."

"Hit away, Syl," he said to Sylvester, who was looking at him for instructions.

The fans yelled wildly as he stepped to the plate. He glanced at the scoreboard: 5 to 5. He'd try to sock another out of the ball park — if he could.

The pitch. It was low, but not too low. He swung. Missed!

"Oh, no!" groaned Terry.

The next pitch was wide.

"Ball one!"

Then, "Stri —" the umpire started to say, but didn't finish. Sylvester had swung at the pitch, and the ball was soaring like a loose balloon out toward deep center field. The Wildcat fielder raced out to the fence, then stood there and watched the ball sail over his head.

For the third time that day Sylvester Coddmyer III trotted around the bases, not slowing down his pace till he crossed home plate. He was given the usual reception from the coach and players, and applause from the fans and cheerleaders.

Bongo, apparently shaken by Sylvester's third homer, walked the next two batters. The next two got out. Then Terry singled, scoring Jerry, and Bobby Kent grounded out to short.

The Wildcats pushed across a run at their turn at bat, but that was all. The Redbirds came out on the big end, 7 to 6.

There was more than just yelling, hand-shaking, and back-patting this time. A photographer from the *Hooper Star* took pictures of Sylvester, and a *Star* reporter, carrying a small tape recorder in one hand and a microphone in the other, popped questions at him. He was never so embar-rassed in his life.

"Is your name really Sylvester Coddmyer the third?"

"Yes."

"How many years have you played baseball, Sylvester?"

"I never played before."

"Are you sure?"

"I'm sure."

"Then how do you account for getting a
home run every time you bat?"

"I just hit the ball squarely on the nose."

"Yes, but — no one else in the world hits a
home run every time up. Do you think there
is something . . . well, uh . . . unusual about
you, Sylvester?"

"No. Why should there be?"

The reporter shrugged. "Well, there
shouldn't." He grinned faintly. "What other
sports are you interested in, Sylvester?"

"No other sport."

"Okay, Sylvester. Thanks very much."

The reporter and photographer left, and
he breathed a sigh of relief. He had barely

relaxed when someone nudged his elbow. "Hi, Sylvester."

It was Snooky Malone, grinning that funny grin of his. He was carrying a small booklet, something about "Your Horoscope." Sylvester wasn't able to see the whole title.

"What's it now, Snooky?" he asked, becoming a little annoyed with Snooky's pestering him.

"Being a Gemini makes you have more ability than the average person, Sylvester," said Snooky proudly.

"Thanks, Snooky," replied Sylvester. "But I haven't got time to listen to that stuff now. I'm tired."

He started for home, and Snooky hopped alongside of him. "This book says that you are ruled by the planet Mercury," Snooky went on. "It also says that when the planet Venus, or the Moon, draws close to Mercury as they are seen from Earth, a Gemini's powers are sharpened. That's why you knock home runs every time you bat, Sylvester."

"I'm glad to hear that," said Sylvester, not very impressed.

"But that's not the only reason why."

Sylvester stared at the big periods behind Snooky's glasses. "What do you mean by that?"

"I read quite a lot about paranormal events, too."

"Paranormal?" Sylvester frowned, perplexed. "What's that?"

The dark eyes held onto his unflinchingly. "It means out-of-the-ordinary, unexplainable, mysterious," said Snooky. He paused, as if to give time for that information to sink in. "Who do you keep looking at and waving to in the bleachers behind first base, Sylvester?"

"George Baruth. Why?"

"George Baruth? Who's he?"

"A friend."

"From around here?"

Sylvester shrugged. "No. He's vacationing here."

"Oh?"

Sylvester looked at him again, then plunged on ahead, determined this time not to stop. "Sorry, Snooky, but I can't hang around any longer."

"See you again, Sylvester," said Snooky.

*Don't be in a hurry about it,* thought Sylvester.

# 10

The Redbirds and the Macon Falcons clashed on the eighth. It seemed that the poor Falcons didn't have enough nourishment even to flutter their wings, let alone play baseball. They crumbled under the Redbirds' attack, 11 to 1.

Sylvester Coddmyer III was up to bat four times and knocked four home runs to keep his streak unbroken. He had nine runs batted in and three put-outs.

"I marked down a home run for you the last time up even before you batted, Syl," said the scorekeeper, proudly.

"Don't you think that's going a little bit too far?" said Sylvester.

There was no school on Monday, the eighteenth. It was Teachers Conference Day. Two hours before game time against the Teaburg Giants, Sylvester Coddmyer III was on his way home with a load of groceries when a combined sound of running footsteps and a high-pitched voice thundered in his ears.

"Hi, Sylvester!" greeted Snooky Malone, coming up beside him and grinning that elfish grin of his.

"Hi, Snooky," said Sylvester, and made a face. "You're not going to start on that horoscope and paranormal stuff again, are you?"

"As a matter of fact" — Snooky paused — "I was. But not here."

"Good," said Sylvester, and picked up speed.

Snooky grabbed his arm. "At Chris an'

Greens, Sylvester. I want to treat you to a delicious pie à la mode."

Sylvester slowed down to almost a stop. "Pie à la mode?" His mouth watered. "Pie à la mode's my favorite dessert."

Snooky's smile was almost fiendish. "I know." He coaxed Sylvester to the corner and across the street to Chris an' Greens, Sylvester fighting against the impulse every step of the way. It was a losing battle, and the way he tackled the pie à la mode he didn't mind having lost at all.

"We're friends, aren't we, Sylvester?" said Snooky, taking an occasional sip of his lemonade.

Sylvester looked at him. "If I didn't know you, Snooky, I'd think you were trying to sell me something."

Snooky laughed. "All I want you to do is trust me," he said.

"Who said I didn't?"

"Okay. Tell me your secret. George Baruth is no real person, is he? He's someone you've made up."

"Snooky, you've got bats in your head. He's as real as you are."

"No, he isn't. He's a figment of your imagination."

Sylvester stared at him. "Snooky," he said, "I'm beginning to think that *you're* a figment of my imagination!"

"That's because I'm different from most kids," smiled Snooky.

"You can say that again," said Sylvester. He turned to what was left of the pie à la mode and finished it.

"Want more?" asked Snooky. "I've been saving up my allowance for a new book on astrology, but I can wait another week."

The thought of eating another pie à la

mode hit Sylvester like a sledgehammer. "You sure it's okay?" he asked.

"I wouldn't ask you if it weren't," answered Snooky, and he ordered another pie à la mode for Sylvester.

For a while both boys held their silence. Sylvester took his time devouring his second pie à la mode; Snooky took his time sipping his first lemonade.

*Snooky must have bats in his head,* thought Sylvester sourly. Saying that George Baruth wasn't real was plain ridiculous.

"I've got an idea," said Snooky, the smile on his face broadening. "How about introducing me to him this afternoon at the game?"

"Sure. Why not?"

Suddenly he didn't feel good. He was full of pie à la mode — so full his stomach was beginning to rebel.

"I've got to get home, Snooky," he said,

sliding off the stool and grabbing the bag of groceries. "I don't feel good."

"Gee, Sylvester!" cried Snooky. "I hope you're not getting sick!"

"It's too late," muttered Sylvester. "I'm sick already."

He hurried home, plopped the bag of groceries into his mother's arms, and headed directly to his room, where he toppled on the bed, so hot he felt he was burning. His mother came in.

"Sylvester!" she cried. "What's happened to you? Where have you been for the last hour?"

"Snoo — Snooky Malone . . . treated me to . . . two pie à la modes," he said, and moaned.

"Two pie à la modes? No wonder you're sick!" She lifted his feet onto the bed and covered him with a blanket. "You made a pig of yourself. When are you going to learn?"

He moaned again, too sick to answer her. He closed his eyes and heard his mother leave and the door latch click shut.

Sometime later he was awakened from his sleep, and his mother said there were several boys here to see him. "Do you feel better?" she asked. "Or shall I tell them you'll see them tomorrow?"

"I feel better," he said. "Send them in."

She left and a moment later in came Jim Cowley, Terry Barnes and Eddie Exton. "What happened to you?" asked Jim.

"Stuffed myself with pie à la modes," replied Sylvester. "How did the game come out?"

"We lost," said Eddie. "Ten to four."

"It was your fault," said Terry. "You and your pie à la modes." Then he grinned. "Know what? I'm nuts about 'em, too."

There was a change in the lineup when the Seneca Indians played the Redbirds. Coach Corbin moved Sylvester up to fourth in the batting order. Sylvester had been up there before, in a scrimmage game. Would he perform well enough today to earn the position for good?

The Indians were leading by one run when Sylvester came to bat in the bottom of the first inning. Jim Cowley was on first after uncorking a single.

Bert Riley, a tall, loose-jointed kid with a funny way of throwing the ball, was on the mound. He toed the rubber, stretched, and threw. Every part of his body seemed to go into motion before the ball actually left his hand.

The pitch was wide. "Ball!"

Bert went through his peculiar motions again, and pitched. *Pow!* The hit was as solid as it sounded. The ball took off like a shot and cleared the left-field fence by at least twenty feet. The crowd roared, and Sylvester started his slow, easy trot around the bases.

He glanced at the bleachers as he reached first base and saw George Baruth sitting there at the end of the third row, smiling that boyish smile of his. He waved and Sylvester waved back.

Then Sylvester saw the kid sitting next to Mr. Baruth waving to him, too, and he recognized Snooky Malone.

"Nice blast, Sylvester!" Snooky shouted.

*Hm,* thought Sylvester. Apparently Snooky had taken it upon himself to meet George Baruth.

The Indians picked up two runs in the top of the third. Then Sylvester hit his second home run in the bottom of the fourth. Indians 3, Redbirds 3.

As Sylvester ran out to the field, he looked over at George Baruth and Snooky Malone. He expected to see Snooky talking Mr. Baruth's head off. Snooky was busy talking, all right, but it was with the kid on his left side. Maybe Snooky wasn't interested in getting into a conversation with an old guy like Mr. Baruth.

Terry's first pitch was blasted out to deep right, directly at Sylvester. Sylvester sprinted forward a few steps, then suddenly panicked. The ball was hit farther than he expected!

He turned and ran in the opposite direction. His short legs were a blur as he ran. He looked over his left shoulder, then his right. There was the ball, dropping ahead of him!

Somehow he picked up more speed, stretched out his glove hand, and caught the ball.

The applause from the Redbird fans was tremendous. A double between left and center fields braced up the Indians' hopes of scoring, but a pop fly and then a one-hopper to Terry ended the top half of the fifth inning.

Jim, leading off, flied out to center. Ted walked and advanced to second on Milt's single over short. Up came Sylvester Coddmyer III and the Redbird fans went wild again.

The Indians called time. The infielders ran in toward the mound, surrounding their pitcher, Bert Riley. They held a quiet, lengthy discussion, then returned to their positions.

*What now?* thought Sylvester, as Bert Riley faced him for the third time.

"Ball!" shouted the ump, as Bert blazed one in — a mile outside.

"Ball two!" shouted the ump. Another one outside.

"Ball three!" And another.

"He's afraid of you, Syl!" yelled Snooky Malone. "He's gonna walk you!"

And that's just what Bert did. Sylvester was walked his first time ever.

All kinds of noises exploded from the Redbird fans. Some of them yelled. Some of them hissed.

Sylvester didn't care. He didn't get out, that was the important thing.

The bases were loaded, and Jerry Ash was up. The fans and the team gave Jerry all kinds of verbal support, but it did no good. Bert struck him out.

Bobby Kent did a little better. His swinging bat connected with the ball. But the ball hopped up into the Indian shortstop's glove just like a trained rabbit.

The shortstop whipped the ball to second, throwing Sylvester out and ending the Redbirds' threat.

Top of the sixth. A hard blow to short! Milt muffed the ball, picked it up, and pegged it to first. A short throw. Jerry Ash stretched for it. The ball struck the tip of his mitt and rolled aside.

*Oh, come on!* thought Sylvester. *We can't flub the ball now!*

Terry motioned Duane to come in a bit. The third baseman advanced till he was ahead of the bag by a few steps, then bent forward, hands on his knees.

A bunt! Duane rushed in, fielded it, and pegged it to second. Too late! The base umpire's hands fanned out with the "safe" sign. Jim fired to first, but there, too, the hitter beat the throw.

Two on, no outs, and a tied score, 3 and 3.

Terry wiped his forehead, tugged on his

cap, toed the rubber. He stretched, delivered. A blow over second! A run scored! Bobby Kent fielded the ball and threw it in, holding the Indians on third and first.

"Bear down, Terry!" yelled Sylvester.

A smashing grounder down to Jim! He caught the hop, snapped it to Milt. Milt stepped on second, rifled the ball to first. A double play!

Jerry pivoted to throw home, but held up. The Indian on third wasn't taking any chances.

Terry caught the soft throw from Jerry, then climbed to the mound, got Eddie's sign, and pitched. Ball one. He zipped two over the heart of the plate. The Indian batter swung at the first and missed. He blasted the second one over short for a clean single, scoring another run.

Terry struck out the next batter. Indians 5, Redbirds 3.

"Last chance to pull this game out of the fire," said Coach Corbin. "Start it off, Duane. Make 'em be in there."

Duane waited for 'em to be in there and got a two-two count. Bert's next pitch was letter-high, and Duane corked it out to short left field. The Indian outfielder raced in and made a shoestring catch.

Eddie waited for a pitch he liked and blasted it for a single. The hit livened the Redbirds' bench. The players had been sitting there as if their tail feathers had already been clipped.

Terry socked a hard grounder to third, which the baseman caught and pegged to second. The throw was wild!

A cheer exploded from the Redbirds' bench and the cheerleaders as Terry overran first, made his turn, and came back to stand safely on first base.

Then Jim popped up to the catcher for the

second out, and it looked as if the Indians were about to trounce the Redbirds for sure.

Ted Sobel let two strikes go by, then knocked the third pitch between right and center fields for a double! Eddie and Terry scored to tie it up.

What a ball game this was!

Milt walked and once again Sylvester came to the plate.

"Out of the lot, Syl!" shouted Snooky Malone.

A hit out of the lot would mean eight runs and victory. But was Sylvester going to be given the chance to do that? Not if Bert Riley, who had called a time out, and the infielders, who were running toward the mound, were planning the same strategy they had planned before.

"Boooooo!" yelled Snooky Malone.

The discussion around the pitcher's box took only half as long as it did the first time.

The players returned to their positions. Bert Riley toed the rubber, pitched, and the ball zipped wide of the plate.

Bert pitched three more almost in the same spot, and for the second time that day, and in his life, Sylvester walked.

The bases were loaded.

"Your baby, Jerry!" yelled Snooky Malone.

*Crack!* A sock over second base! Ted and Milt scored, and that was it. The game was over. Indians 5, Redbirds 7.

The next morning's *Hooper Star* had an item on the sports page that read:

## REDBIRDS PLAYER CONTINUES SENSATIONAL HITTING STREAK

Sylvester Coddmyer III smashed out two homers and was walked twice to keep his batting record unmarred as the Hooper Redbirds beat the Seneca Indians 7 to 5 in the Valley Junior High School League.

His 1.000 batting average, and a home run each time at bat (except for the two walks), is unprecedented in Hooper Redbirds baseball history.

As a matter of fact, it may possibly be unprecedented in national baseball history.

The least impressed person about this sensational hitting, however, is Sylvester himself.

This week two national magazines printed his picture and write-ups about him. Sylvester's comment:

"I just can't see why they're making all the fuss."

The Hooper Redbirds played the Broton Tigers that evening and took the game, 8 to 4. Sylvester was walked the first time up, hit homers his next two times up. One was a grand-slammer.

Newspaper reporters, photographers, and a television crew from Syracuse made him their center of attention after he had won the game against the Lansing Wildcats practically single-handed. The score was 4 to 0, and he had made all the runs himself — by homers.

"Do you think you'd like to play in the big leagues after you get out of school, Sylvester?" asked a reporter.

"I don't know. I might."

"Do you practice batting a lot? Do you think that's why you keep on hitting home runs?"

"I don't practice any more than the other guys do," replied Sylvester sincerely.

"Do you suppose it's the way you stand at the plate that gives you so much power?"

"Maybe. I never gave it much thought."

He felt a gnawing ache growing in his stomach and forced a smile. "Do — do you mind if we stop now? I'm getting awfully hungry."

"Of course, Sylvester. Thanks very much for your time," said the reporter.

Sylvester started to ease through the crowd, smiling at the many faces smiling at him. He looked for the one he was most anxious to see, and finally saw it near the edge of the crowd.

"Hi, Mr. Baruth," he greeted.

"Hi, Sylvester," said George Baruth. "Boy! Are you a celebrity!"

"Yeah, I guess I am."

"Just make sure you don't get swellheaded from all the fuss," warned George Baruth.

"Swellheaded?" Sylvester looked up at Mr. Baruth with large question marks in his eyes.

"Yes. You know — strutting around like a cocky rooster. Ignoring your friends. Not listening to your mother and father. Thinking you have suddenly become a lot better than other people. That's being swellheaded. It's the worst kind of thing that could happen to a person who becomes famous."

The possibility of his becoming like that frightened Sylvester. "That would be awful, Mr. Baruth. I think I'd rather not play baseball again than get swellheaded."

George Baruth smiled and patted him on the shoulder. "That's the way to talk, son. You're a levelheaded boy."

"Hey, Sylvester!" someone shouted from behind him. "Wait!"

Sylvester recognized the screechy voice even before he turned.

It was Snooky Malone's.

# 13

Ah . . . Sylvester," said George Baruth. "This is where I'll leave you. See you later."

"Okay, Mr. Baruth."

Snooky came pounding up the sidewalk and stopped beside him, smiling broadly.

"Man! What publicity you're getting!" he cried, breathing hard. "Even television! Wow!"

Sylvester shrugged, unimpressed. "I just hope they don't do it too often," he said. "What time is it, Snooky?"

Snooky looked at his wristwatch. "Five-thirty."

"Oh, man! Mom's probably wondering what happened to me!" He started to run. "Sorry, Snooky, but I've got to get home!"

He realized then that George Baruth wasn't ahead of him. Nor was George behind him. He looked back toward the houses he had passed but couldn't see his friend anywhere.

"What are you looking for?" asked Snooky, running along beside him.

"Mr. Baruth," said Sylvester. "He was with me just before you came."

"Mr. Baruth? The man you told me about?"

"Yes."

"He was with you just before I came?"

"Yes. You must have seen him."

Snooky chuckled. "No, I didn't. I didn't see anybody with you, Sylvester."

Sylvester looked at him perplexedly. "You're lying."

"I am not lying."

"But he was with me!"

Snooky smiled mischievously. "I believe you."

Sylvester's jaw dropped. "Why should you if you didn't see him?"

"Because I know you're a Gemini and are ruled by a special Sun Sign that makes it possible for you to see into the beyond."

"You're talking crazy, Snooky," said Sylvester, still staring at the periodlike eyes behind the dark lenses of Snooky's glasses.

"A common response," said Snooky. "But I'm surprised to hear it from you."

"But you've met him!" cried Sylvester. "You were talking to him at the baseball field!"

"Syl, how could I have talked to him when I have never even seen the guy?" said Snooky.

Sylvester's eyes grew wider. "But you were sitting beside him in the bleachers the other day."

"I was? I didn't see anybody I didn't know." Snooky smiled and put a hand on Sylvester's shoulder. "I envy you, Syl. I really do."

They reached the intersection and Snooky paused. "Well, here's where I turn off, Syl. See you later."

"'Bye, Snooky."

*Snooky isn't a bad name for him,* thought Sylvester as he continued up the street alone. *But Snoopy would be more fitting.*

Mom had supper ready, just as Sylvester had figured. She wondered what had delayed him, and he told her. She listened to him, eyes fixed on him.

"It's the truth, Mom," he said. "Every word of it."

"I believe you," she said. "But why you, Sylvester?"

"'Cause I'm the only one who hits a home run every time. And I've been walked only three times."

"And that's unusual?" asked his mother.

He grinned. "Yes, Mom. I guess it is."

Sylvester knocked three home runs against the Macon Falcons on June 3, but the Redbirds lost in spite of it, 7 to 6.

The next morning's *Hooper Star* read:

### REDBIRDS LOSE
### IN SPITE OF
### CODDMYER'S
### THREE HOMERS

Sylvester Coddmyer III's three home runs were not enough to help the Redbirds in their game against the Macon Falcons yesterday. It was the Redbirds' second loss of their first highly successful season, thanks to the powerful bat of Sylvester Coddmyer III.

So far he has compiled a record of twenty-one home runs, an unprecedented record.

He has never struck out nor scored any hits other than home runs, leaving him with a batting average of 1.000.

Asked by this reporter what he makes of the youth's exceptional hitting, Redbirds Coach Stan Corbin says he doesn't know. The fact is, neither does anyone else.

As for Sylvester Coddmyer III, his bat is doing all the talking.

That evening a Mr. Johnson from one of the nation's most popular magazines came to the house and said that his magazine was offering Sylvester fifteen thousand dollars if he would let them publish his biography.

"Since you are under age, one of your

parents would have to sign, too," said Mr. Johnson.

Sylvester and his mother seemed paralyzed for a while. They stood staring at the man like wax figures.

Mr. Johnson smiled. "Of course, there will be more money coming to you from other sources," he said. "We are thinking of sponsoring an hour special on a television network and taking you to New York for an appearance on two or three national television shows. You and your husband may go along with him, of course, Mrs. Coddmyer, with all expenses paid."

"We . . . we may?"

That was all Mrs. Coddmyer could say. As for Sylvester, he was unable to say anything. Just listen. He wasn't sure whether this was all real or just a dream.

"What do you think, Mom?" he asked after he realized that Mr. Johnson was waiting for an answer.

"What? Oh — I think it's absolutely fine." Her eyes bounced worriedly back and forth between Sylvester and Mr. Johnson. "It'd help to pay up our bills, wouldn't it?"

"Part of the money will be put in a trust fund for Sylvester's education," explained Mr. Johnson.

"Oh, yes, of course," said Mrs. Coddmyer. She was sitting down now and twisting a napkin round and round on her lap.

Mr. Johnson placed a couple of sheets of paper on the table. "This is the contract binding you and our company," he explained. "I'll leave it with you to read over thoroughly at your convenience. You may want to have your lawyer read it."

"We don't have a lawyer," said Mrs. Coddmyer.

"You really don't need one. But read over the contract before you sign it. I assure you it contains all I have discussed with you and that it is perfectly legitimate."

"Oh, we're sure of that, Mr. Johnson," said Mrs. Coddmyer.

Mr. Johnson smiled, rose, and shook hands with them. "I'll telephone in a day or two," he said, and left.

Sylvester sat thinking hard. All these great things happening to him were not just by accident. He had been helped, and the person who had helped him was his friend George Baruth.

If anyone was able to offer advice it was Mr. Baruth. Dad wasn't home, anyway. He wouldn't be for almost a week.

"I know who we can ask for advice, Mom," said Sylvester. "He's not a lawyer, but I know he'd be glad to give us advice about this."

"We should ask your father, Sylvester."

"Oh, Mom! He won't be home for almost a week! And he usually agrees with you on important things, anyway!"

"Who's this man you're talking about, Sylvester?"

"George Baruth. That friend of mine I told you about."

Mom groaned. "George Baruth? Sylvester, are you sure you know what you're saying? I've heard you talk about him, yes. But I have never seen the man, nor have I ever heard of him except from you."

"I don't care, Mom" said Sylvester seriously. "He's a great guy and he's my friend. And he helped me become what I am. I know he'll be glad to help us on this."

Mom sighed. "Okay, if you say so. Do you know his phone number?"

"He's on vacation here. But I'll see him."

**H**e was returning from school the next day when who should he meet coming toward him from Winslow Street but George Baruth himself.

"Good afternoon, kid," said George. "Fancy meeting you."

"Yeah," said Sylvester. Excitement suddenly overwhelmed him. "Got something very important to ask you, Mr. Baruth," he said.

"Oh? What?"

"Mr. Johnson, from a famous magazine, was at our house last evening and left a contract for me to sign," said Sylvester. "He says that his company wants to publish my biography and will pay me a lot of money for it. They'll also put money into a trust fund for my education. And I'll be on TV shows, and Mom and Dad can come along with all expenses paid. Mr. Johnson says we can have our lawyer read the contract before we sign it, because either Mom or Dad has to sign it, too. But we don't have a lawyer."

He paused to catch his breath.

"And you'd like me to read the contract and advise you on what to do. Is that it?" asked George Baruth.

Sylvester's head bobbed like a cork on a wavy sea.

"Well," said George Baruth, starting down the street, Sylvester pacing beside him like a pup, "I don't know for sure what to say myself."

"Don't you want to read the contract?"

"I don't have to. I know what it says. You told me. It's honest, that's for sure. As for signing it . . ." He halted and looked at Sylvester with a deep, haunting look in his eyes Sylvester had not ever seen before.

"It's a lot of publicity and money, Sylvester. But fame could be a dangerous thing. It could ruin one's life. The first taste of it is sweet. So you'd want more. It's human nature. But something bad could happen. Suppose your hitting dropped to rock bottom? People would laugh at you. Your own friends would mock you. You'd wish you'd never seen a baseball."

Mr. Baruth paused, took out a handkerchief, and wiped his face.

"Something else about it bothers me, too," he said.

"What, Mr. Baruth?"

"Well . . . me. What I did to make you into

a great baseball hitter. You see, Syl," suddenly his eyes looked dim and sad, "I won't be around much longer. And, with me gone, you may not be hitting like you used to. . . ." He paused.

"I'll sure miss you, Mr. Baruth."

"And I'll miss you."

"Then you . . . you don't think I should sign the contract?"

George Baruth eyed him silently for a long while, then said, "Suppose you decide that yourself, Syl?"

Sylvester shrugged. "Okay. Thanks, Mr. Baruth. You've been awfully kind to me."

"You've been a joy to me, too, Syl."

They shook hands.

"Will you be at the next game?"

"You bet," said George Baruth.

Sylvester turned, started to run, and bumped into Snooky Malone, hitting the little guy so hard that Snooky fell to the sidewalk, his glasses falling off and his books spilling out of his hands.

"Hey, watch it!" yelled Snooky.

"Oh, sorry, Snooky!" cried Sylvester. "I didn't see you!"

"I guess you didn't!" exclaimed Snooky, rising to his feet.

Sylvester picked up the glasses, handed them to the little guy, then gathered up the books.

"I heard you talking," said Snooky.

Sylvester looked at the huge periods behind the glasses. "What did I say?"

"'Thanks, Mr. Baruth. You've been awfully kind to me. Will you be at the next game?'"

"That's all?"

Snooky nodded, and smiled. "You were talking with George Baruth, weren't you?"

Sylvester nodded. Darn Snooky, snooping around all the time.

"What were you talking about?"

"Something very important, but I can't tell you about it, Snooky. Sorry."

He and Mom talked a lot about the contract that night. Mr. Johnson called the next morning and arrived that afternoon. He looked at the contract and frowned.

"It's not signed," he observed.

"No, it isn't," said Sylvester. "We decided it was best that I didn't."

"Why, Sylvester? Isn't the money enough?"

"Oh, it's not the money, Mr. Johnson. It's just that I don't deserve it and all that publicity. I'd be thinking about it all my life, and I wouldn't want to do that. I'm sorry, Mr. Johnson, but that's how Mom and I decided."

# 15

The Hooper Redbirds beat the Teaburg Giants 8 to 3 on June 8, leaving one more game to play for the Redbirds. Sylvester's home-run streak went unbroken. He had three in three times up, twice with no runners on, once with two on. Mr. Baruth was at the game, sitting in his usual place.

Immediately after the game, and all the way home, Snooky Malone clung to Sylvester like a leech. Now and then Sylvester looked around for George Baruth but didn't see him. Was he staying away because of snoopy Snooky? Probably.

It wasn't till the next day after supper, while Sylvester was brooding about George Baruth on the front porch steps, that Mr. Baruth stopped by.

"Oh, hi, Mr. Baruth!" Sylvester greeted him happily.

"Hi, kid," said Geor~ ⁓ contract?"

"No, sir. M( decided agains

"Did you tell

"Of course. 1 Mr. Baruth?"

George Barut someone had turi ⁓ ⁓ ıım. "Sure it was all rig..t. ıt's all right all the way down the line, kid." He paused. "Well, good-bye, kid. And keep happy, hear?"

Sylvester nodded, and stood up. "Are you — are you leaving now, Mr. Baruth?" he asked.

The big man nodded and walked down the street, head bowed, till he was out of sight.

The crowd on Thursday was the biggest ever. People filled the grandstand and the bleachers, and were lying down or standing behind both foul lines. The game was against the Seneca Indians, and the Redbirds had first raps.

Left-handed Bert Riley was on the mound again for the Indians and walked the first three men up. For a while no one was advancing toward the plate, and Coach Corbin said, "Sylvester, wake up."

Sylvester rose from the on-deck circle and walked to the plate. He had been looking at the end of the third-row bleacher seats — looking for George Baruth. But, for the first time since the season had started, George Baruth wasn't there.

"Steerike!" yelled the ump as Bert blazed in a pitch.

"Ball!"

"Ball two!"

Then, "Strike two!"

Sylvester stepped out of the box, wiped his face with his sleeve, and stepped in again. Tensely, he waited for the next pitch. The crowd was hushed. Bert stretched, delivered. The throw looked good. Sylvester leaned into it and swung.

*Plop!* sounded the ball as it struck the catcher's mitt. The next second the crowd roared and it was as if a gigantic bomb had exploded. Sylvester Coddmyer III had struck out.

He walked to the bench, his head bowed.

"Don't worry about it, Syl!" yelled a familiar voice. "You'll bat again!" It sounded like Snooky Malone.

Jerry Ash flied out. Then Bobby Kent

singled, scoring two runs, and Duane Francis grounded out.

The Indians scored once, and that was it till the fourth inning, when Eddie Exton doubled and came in on Terry Barnes's neat single over first base.

The Indians made up for the run and more besides. With two men on, a left-handed hitter socked a clothesline drive out to right field. The ball grazed the top of Sylvester's glove and bounced out to the fence. Sylvester ran as hard as he could after it, picked it up, and heaved it in.

Three runs scored. The Indians tallied four runs that half inning, going ahead, 5 to 3.

Sylvester led off in the top of the fifth. He had looked once more for George Baruth in the seat at the end of the third row, hoping to see him. But the big man wasn't there.

Not until now was he sure that he would never see his friend again.

He struck out on three straight pitches.

Jerry doubled, though, and Bobby knocked him in for the Redbirds' only run that half inning.

Back bounced the Indians for three more runs to make their score 8. And back came the Redbirds for their last chance.

Jim walked. Ted singled. Milt flied out. And up came Sylvester.

"Knock it over the fence, Syl!" yelled Snooky Malone.

The pitch. Sylvester swung. *Crack!* A hit! But not one of those long ones that he had been hitting all season. Not an over-the-fence blast that made the crowd draw in its collective breath.

It was a shallow drive but hard, with the ball rolling between the left and center fielders. Two runs scored and Sylvester reached second base for a double, the only hit he had made all season that wasn't a home run.

Both Jerry and Bobby got out, and that was it. The Indians won, 8 to 6.

He thought it was all over then. He thought the people had suddenly forgotten him. But they hadn't. They crowded around him, patting him on the back and shaking his hand while photographers snapped pictures like crazy.

Then someone pushed through the crowd, and a silence fell like a curtain.

"Sylvester," said Coach Stan Corbin, standing there with a huge, bright trophy of a boy swinging a baseball bat, "in honor of our school, Hooper Junior High, and all the teachers and students and myself, I am happy to present this trophy to the greatest athlete Hooper Junior High School has ever had."

So choked up that he was unable to say a word, Sylvester accepted the trophy. Finally he was able to speak.

"Thanks," he said.

His mother and Snooky Malone walked on either side of him as he carried the trophy home.

But, somehow, it seemed that the trophy wasn't quite as heavy as it was when the coach had given it to him. It seemed lighter, as if someone else was helping him carry it.

## FINAL STANDINGS

|           | WON | LOST |
|-----------|-----|------|
| Redbirds  | 7   | 3    |
| Giants    | 6   | 4    |
| Wildcats  | 6   | 4    |
| Tigers    | 5   | 5    |
| Falcons   | 4   | 6    |
| Indians   | 3   | 7    |

★ ★ ★ ★ ★ ★ ★ ★ ★ ★ ★ ★ ★ ★ ★ ★ ★ ★ ★ ★ ★ ★ ★ ★ ★

★

# READ ALL THE BOOKS

### In The

### New MATT CHRISTOPHER Sports Library!

**THE BASKET COUNTS**
978-1-59953-212-7

**CATCH THAT PASS!**
978-1-59953-105-2

**CENTER COURT STING**
978-1-59953-106-9

**THE COMEBACK CHALLENGE**
978-1-59953-211-0

**DIRT BIKE RACER**
978-1-59953-113-7

**DIRT BIKE RUNAWAY**
978-1-59953-215-8

**THE GREAT QUARTERBACK SWITCH**
978-1-59953-216-5

**THE HOCKEY MACHINE**
978-1-59953-214-1

**ICE MAGIC**
978-1-59953-112-0

**THE KID WHO ONLY HIT HOMERS**
978-1-59953-107-6

**LONG-ARM QUARTERBACK**
978-1-59953-114-4

**MOUNTAIN BIKE MANIA**
978-1-59953-108-3

**RETURN OF THE HOME RUN KID**
978-1-59953-213-4

**SKATEBOARD TOUGH**
978-1-59953-115-1

**SNOWBOARD MAVERICK**
978-1-59953-116-8

**SNOWBOARD SHOWDOWN**
978-1-59953-109-0

**SOCCER HALFBACK**
978-1-59953-110-6

**SOCCER SCOOP**
978-1-59953-117-5

★ ★ ★ ★ ★ ★ ★ ★ ★ ★ ★ ★ ★ ★ ★ ★ ★ ★ ★ ★ ★ ★ ★ ★ ★